For Kian, Louis, Wayne and Terry

First published in 2011 by Macmillan Children's Books
This edition published 2012 by Macmillan Children's Books
a division of Macmillan Publishers Limited
20 New Wharf Road, London N1 9RR
Basingstoke and Oxford
www.panmacmillan.com
Associated companies worldwide
ISBN 978-0-330-54403-0
Text and Illustrations copyright © Emily Gravett, 2011
The right of Emily Gravett to be identified as the Author and Illustrator
of this work has been asserted in accordance
with the Copyright, Designs and Patents Act 1988
All rights reserved.
No part of this publication may be reproduced
or transmitted in any form, or by any means without permission.

1 3 5 7 9 8 6 4 2

A CIP catalogue record for this book is available from the British Library
Printed in China

AGAIN

Emily Gravett

MACMILLAN CHILDREN'S BOOKS

For Kian, Louis, Wayne and Terry

First published in 2011 by Macmillan Children's Books
This edition published 2012 by Macmillan Children's Books
a division of Macmillan Publishers Limited
20 New Wharf Road, London N1 9RR
Basingstoke and Oxford
www.panmacmillan.com
Associated companies worldwide
ISBN 978-0-330-54403-0

1 3 5 7 9 8 6 4 2

A CIP catalogue record for this book is available from the British Library
Printed in China

AGAIN!

Emily Gravett

MACMILLAN CHILDREN'S BOOKS

It was nearly bedtime.

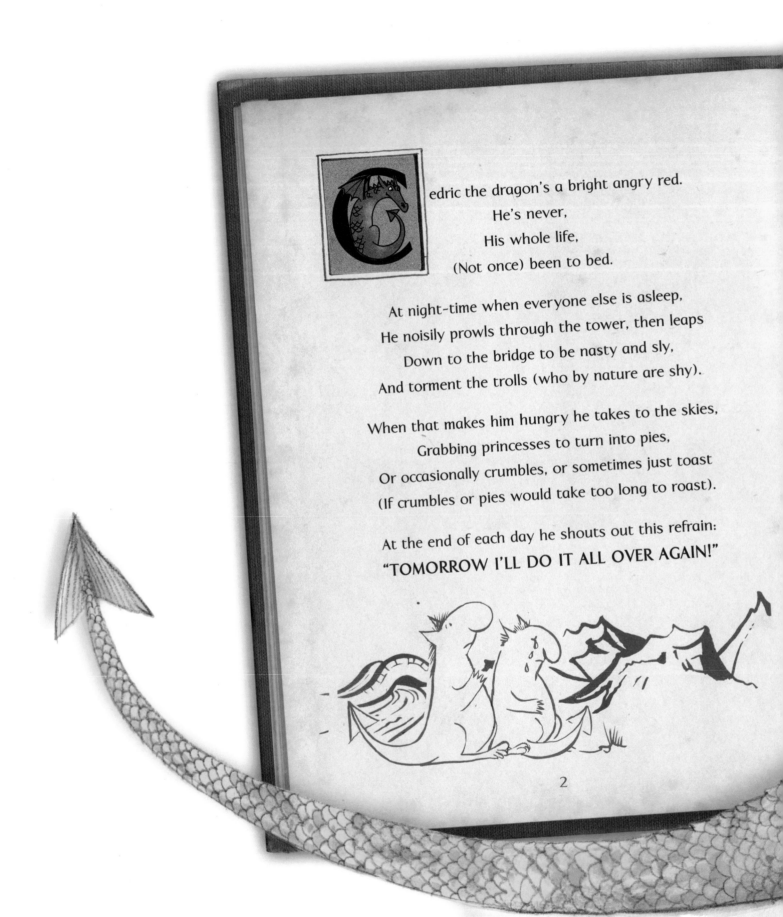

edric the dragon's a bright angry red.
He's never,
His whole life,
(Not once) been to bed.

At night-time when everyone else is asleep,
He noisily prowls through the tower, then leaps
Down to the bridge to be nasty and sly,
And torment the trolls (who by nature are shy).

When that makes him hungry he takes to the skies,
Grabbing princesses to turn into pies,
Or occasionally crumbles, or sometimes just toast
(If crumbles or pies would take too long to roast).

At the end of each day he shouts out this refrain:
"TOMORROW I'LL DO IT ALL OVER AGAIN!"

Again?

Cedric the dragon's a bright angry red.
He's never,
His whole life,
(Not once) been to bed.

At night-time when Cedric SHOULD be asleep,
He noisily stomps through the tower, then leaps
Down to the bridge to say a big sorry
For teasing the trolls (who do tend to worry).

When that makes him hungry he takes out a pie
Which he shares with the trolls. Then, heaving a sigh,
He goes home to his tower
And shouts out this refrain:
"TOMORROW I'LL DO IT ALL OVER AGAIN!"

3

AGAIN!

Cedric the dragon's a big sleepyhead.
He's decided it's time
HE WAS REALLY IN BED.

He's made friends with the princess
And wished her goodnight,
The trolls are all happy,
The moon is out bright.

Now I'm closing the book and saying quite plain:

"TOMORROW I'll read it all over again."

2

AGAIN!

AGAIN!

Cedric the dragon is no longer red,
As Cedric . . .
the dragon's . . . asleep
. . . in . . . his . . . be . . . z z z z

AGAIN!
AGAIN!
AGAIN!

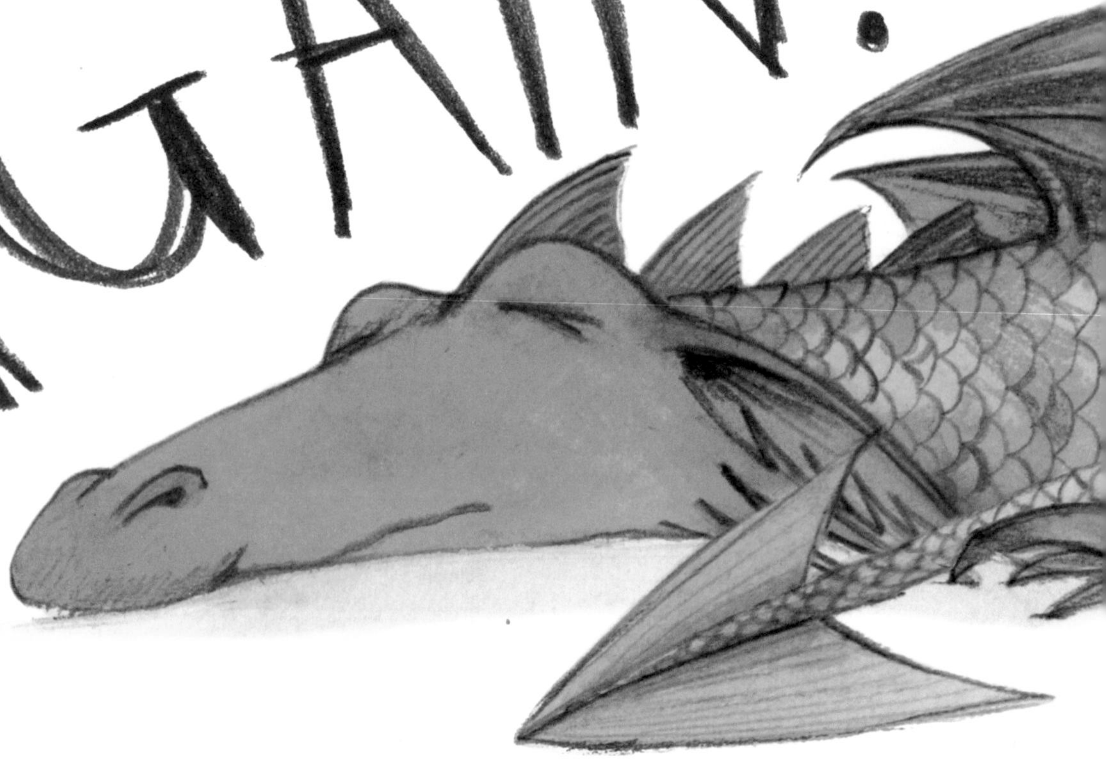

AGAIN! AGAIN AGAIN

AGAIN

AGAIN AGAIN

AGAIN

AGAIN!

At the end of each day he shouts out this refrain:
"TOMORROW I'LL DO IT ALL OVER AGAIN!"

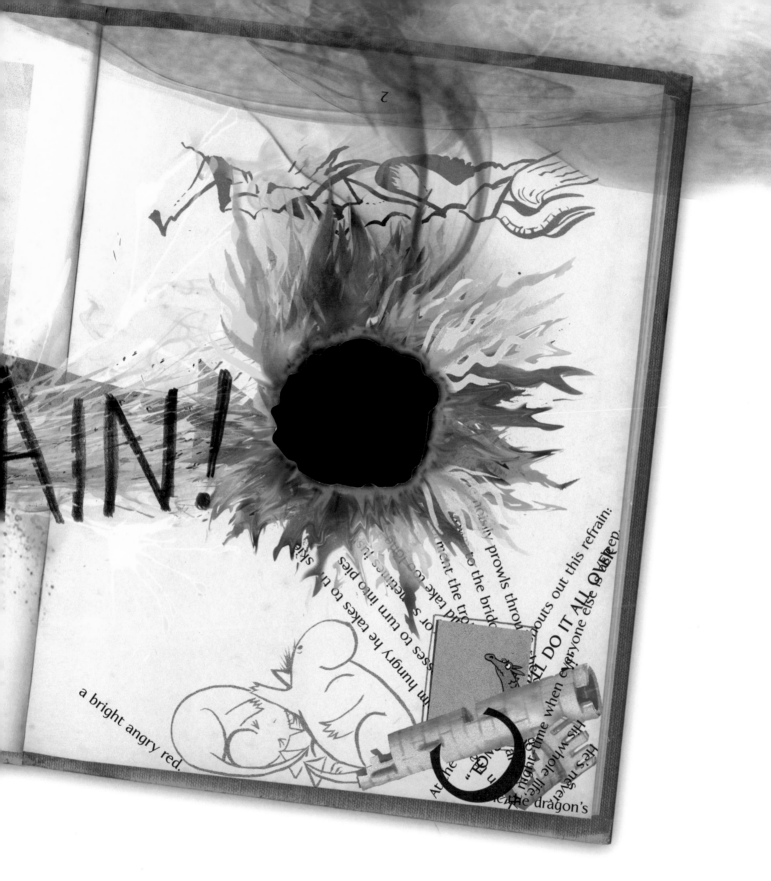

AIN!

a bright angry red.

I'm hungry he takes to tu...
sses to turn into pies
or's metimes just...

...prowls throu...
...the bride...
...the tro...
...shouts out this refrain:

'LL DO IT ALL OVER...

At the...
He's ne...
...when everyone else...
His whole life...
...the dragon's

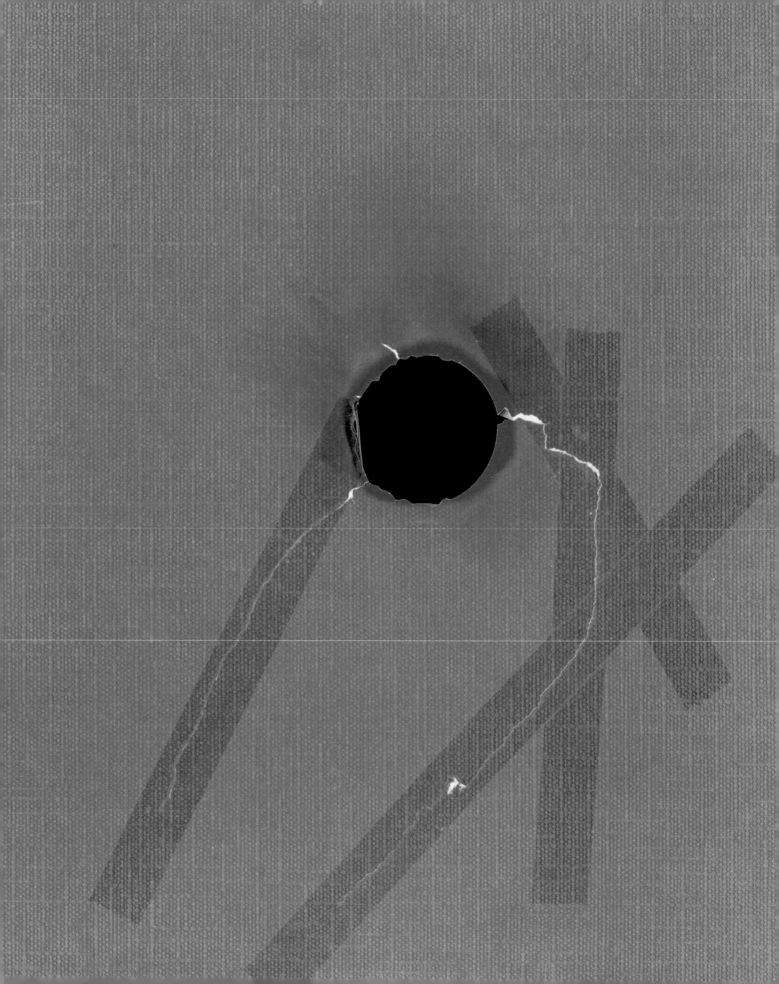

For Deborah
~ DB

For my daughter, Kirsten
~ GH

LITTLE TIGER PRESS LTD,
an imprint of the Little Tiger Group
1 Coda Studios, 189 Munster Road, London SW6 6AW
www.littletiger.co.uk
First published in Great Britain 2001
This edition published 2017
Text copyright © David Bedford 2001
Illustrations copyright © Gaby Hansen 2001
David Bedford and Gaby Hansen have asserted their rights to be identified as the author
and illustrator of this work under the Copyright, Designs and Patents Act, 1988
All rights reserved • ISBN 978-1-84869-783-6
Printed in China • LTP/2700/2736/0319
10 9 8 7 6 5 4 3 2

by David Bedford
Illustrated by Gaby Hansen

Big Bears Can!

LITTLE TiGER
LONDON

Big Bear had to look after
Little Bear when Mother
Bear went out.
"Do I have to?" asked
Big Bear.
"Yes," said Mother Bear.
"Just keep the house neat.
I won't be long."

"What can Big Bears do?" asked Little Bear
when Mother Bear had gone.
"Big Bears can do *everything*," said Big Bear.
"Can they stand on their heads?"
"Yes they can," said Big Bear.

This Little Tiger book belongs to:

_____

_____

_____

"See!"

"But they can't do *this*," said Little Bear . . .

BOING! BOING!
"Of course they can,"
said Big Bear.
"That's easy."

BOING, BOING, BOING...

"Oops!"

"Can you fix the springs?"
asked Little Bear.
"Yes," said Big Bear.
"I can."

"But you can't do *this*,"
said Little Bear. "No way."

"Big Bears don't swing," said Big Bear. "That would be silly." "You're too big to swing, anyway," said Little Bear.

"NO I'M NOT," roared Big Bear. "Watch this!"

"Look out!"
said Little Bear.
"You're too heavy!"

"You've squashed the flowers, too," said Little Bear. "Can you fix everything?"
"I *hope* I can," said Big Bear.

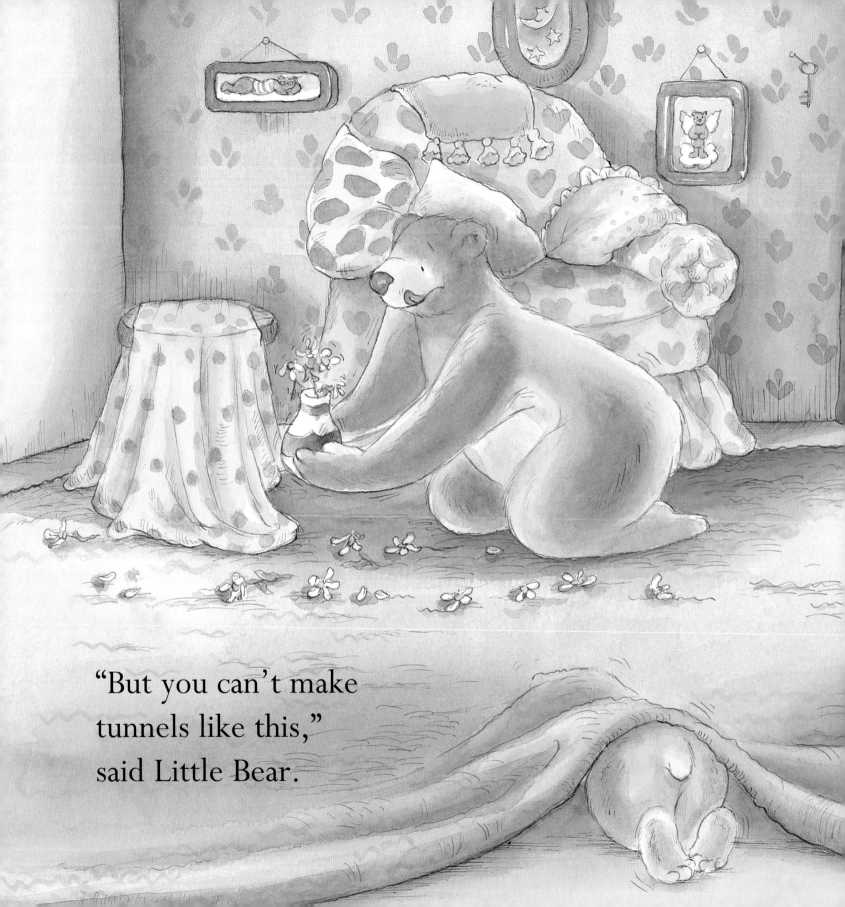

"But you can't make
tunnels like this,"
said Little Bear.

"I don't want to make tunnels," said Big Bear. "I'm going to sit quietly until Mother Bear comes back."

"Big Bears *can't* do everything," sang Little Bear. "Big Bears *can't*, Big Bears *can't*, Big Bears CAN'T do everything." "YES THEY CAN!" said Big Bear.

"This is fun, isn't it?" said Big Bear.
"HERE COMES MOTHER BEAR," shouted
Little Bear. "She's going to be very angry."

"Big Bears can't hide," said
Little Bear.
"Yes they can," said Big
Bear. "Move over so I can
squeeze in beside you."
"There's not enough room,"
said Little Bear. "Mother
Bear will see you."

"Look at her face," said Little Bear.
"She's very, very, VERY angry."
"Big Bears can't get told off," whispered
Big Bear. "Can they?"

YES THEY CAN!

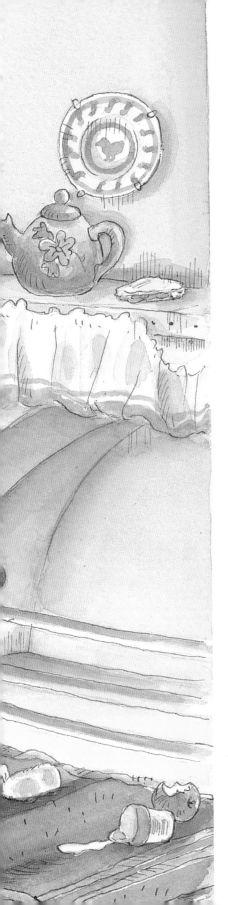

Poor Big Bear. If only Little Bear
could make him feel better.
"Can Big Bears have hugs?" asked
Little Bear.

"Yes," said Big Bear.

"Big Bears can!"